Funny Teeth and Bunny Ears

Written by Dr. Humairah Shah
Illustrations by Adriana Clark

This Book Belongs to:

Charlie and his twin sister, Marlie, were six years old and they both loved to suck their thumbs. Their mother kept telling them to stop, but they just wouldn't do it.

"You are going to turn into bunnies if you don't stop that", scolded their mother. But Charlie and Marlie didn't believe her and just laughed. Marlie whispered to Charlie, "How silly! We're not going to turn into bunnies just because we suck our thumbs!"

Just as their mother had warned them, their bodies slowly began to change. Their teeth began to stick out and look funny and their ears grew bigger and bigger. Finally one day, they did turn into bunnies! Pink-nosed, long eared, cottontails!

At first, it didn't bother Charlie and Marlie at all. They were quite excited about being bunnies and would happily hop around the park or play in the backyard all day long. They made new bunny friends and their mother built them a cozy, little hutch in the backyard. "This is fun!" boasted Charlie.

But, after some time, they began to feel lonely. Charlie missed playing soccer with his friends and Marlie missed the fun times she and her friends would have dressing up like princesses. Charlie and Marlie didn't want to be bunnies anymore. If only they had taken their mother's advice.

Cuddled up and hidden under a large bush, they both began to cry. "What are we going to do, Marlie?" cried Charlie. "We can't stay like this all our lives." And as soon as those words slipped out of his mouth, a beautiful fairy appeared!

"Why are you both so sad?" asked the fairy. Charlie and Marlie told the fairy their whole story. "Our parents were right, but we didn't listen," said Charlie.

"So, have you learned your lesson?" asked the fairy. Charlie and Marlie nodded their heads eagerly. "Alright then," said the fairy and with a wave of her magic wand, she turned them back into children again. Charlie and Marlie couldn't believe it! They were so happy and promised the fairy that they would never suck their thumbs again.

Waving good-bye to the fairy, Charlie and Marlie raced home. How surprised and happy their parents were to see them! They told their mother and father all about the fairy.

Charlie and Marlie asked their parents to help them. So that night, at bedtime their mom put a big bandage on their thumbs and their dad wrapped up their elbows too...just in case. They also put up a picture in their room from their days as bunnies to help them quit thumb sucking. It was fun to be a bunny...but how much more fun it is
to be a boy and a girl!

No more thumb-sucking!

Month

Sunday	Monday	Tuesday	Wednesday	Thursday	Friday	Saturday

Fill out what month you want to begin to stop sucking your thumb! Every day you go without sucking your thumb is a *gigantic* success! For every 5 days, give yourself a reward!

Instead of sucking my thumb, I did this:

_____

_____

_____

_____

Month

Sunday	Monday	Tuesday	Wednesday	Thursday	Friday	Saturday

Instead of sucking my thumb, I did this:

_____

_____

_____

_____

_____

_____

Other Books by the Author

Leila and the Tooth Fairy is a story that every parent would love to read to their kids when they lose their teeth. The book allows them to save the dates each time they lose a tooth. The story takes the kids to a magical Tooth Fairy Land, and in a fun and easy way educates them about eating a healthy diet.

Leila's First Visit to the Dentist prepares children for their very first dental examination. It is a story that is intended to eliminate the fear of the unknown and make the trip to the dental office more enjoyable.

Sam and the Sugar Bug is a story that educates children about the importance of brushing their teeth. The book also prepares children for having their teeth cared for by a dentist in a fun and engaging way.

Leila and the Tooth Fairy

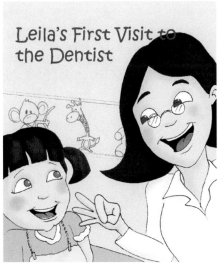

Leila's First Visit to the Dentist

Sam and the Sugar Bug

by Dr. Humairah Shah
Illustrated by Javier Gonzalez III

Listen to your parents...

Made in the USA
Monee, IL
21 April 2021